Molly the Great Tells the Truth:

A Book About Honesty

by Shelley Marshall   Illustrated by Ben Mahan

Molly the Great is having trouble being honest.
What should she do? Let's read!

Enslow Elementary

an imprint of

Enslow Publishers, Inc.

40 Industrial Road
Box 398
Berkeley Heights, NJ 07922
USA

http://www.enslow.com

Molly and Ben are singing.

"Jump to the jungle, the jungle, the jungle …"

It is so fun to bounce on the couch!

The music is so loud. Molly's dad is shouting.
"No bouncing on the couch!"

Molly's dad leaves the room. Molly looks at Ben. They start bouncing again.

They sing, "Where the lucky lion lives, lives, lives!"

Oh no! Molly falls down. She lands on something.
"My crown is broken!"

"What if my Dad finds out?" Molly says. "He will know we were bouncing on the couch."

"I know what to do!" Ben says. He helps Molly hide her crown.

Dad calls, "Do you two want to come to the store?"

"Yes," say Molly and Ben.

"Get your crown," says Molly's dad. "Someone in the store might need your help."

13

"My crown is broken," Molly says.

"How did it break?" asks Dad.

"Ummm," Molly says. "I fell."

"How?" asks Molly's dad.

"I tripped," lies Molly.

18

"What did you trip on?" asks Molly's dad. "Was it the couch?"

Molly is surprised. "How did you know?"

"Tell me what happened," says Molly's dad.

"I was bouncing on the couch," Molly says. "I fell, and my crown broke."

"I am sad that you did not listen to me," says Molly's dad. "But I am more sad that you did not tell me the truth."

"I am sorry, Dad," says Molly. "I will tell the truth from now on."

"Me too!" says Ben.

Dad laughs. "Let's go get some tape to fix that crown!"

23

Read More About Being Honest

Books

Finn, Carrie. *Kids Talk About Honesty*. Minneapolis, MN: Picture Window Books, 2006.

Rankin, Laura. *Ruthie and the (Not So) Teeny Tiny Lie*. New York: Bloomsbury Children's Books, 2007.

Web Site

Kids Next Door

www.hud.gov/kids/people.html

Enslow Elementary, an imprint of Enslow Publishers, Inc.

Enslow Elementary® is a registered trademark of Enslow Publishers, Inc.

Library of Congress Cataloging-in-Publication Data
Marshall, Shelley, 1968-
  Molly the Great tells the truth : a book about honesty / Shelley Marshall.
    p. cm. — (Character education with Super Ben and Molly the Great)
  ISBN 978-0-7660-3520-1
  1. Honesty—Juvenile literature. I. Title.
  BJ1533.H7M37 2010
  179'.9—dc22
                          2009013109

ISBN-13: 978-0-7660-3745-8 (paperback edition)

Printed in the United States of America

092009 Lake Book Manufacturing, Inc., Melrose Park, IL

10 9 8 7 6 5 4 3 2 1

To Our Readers: We have done our best to make sure all Internet Addresses in this book were active and appropriate when we went to press. However, the author and the publisher have no control and assume no liability for the material available on those Internet sites or on other Web sites they may link to. Any comments or suggestions can be sent by e-mail to comments@enslow.com or to the address on the back cover.

♻ Enslow Publishers, Inc. is committed to printing our books on recycled paper. The paper in every book contains 10% to 30% post-consumer waste (PCW). The cover board on the outside of every book contains 100% PCW. Our goal is to do our part to help young people and the environment too!